*by Michael Palmer*

Plan of the City of O (1971)
Blake's Newton (1972)
C's Songs (1973)
Six Poems (1973)
The Circular Gates (1974) 4
Without Music (1977)

Michael Palmer

# *WITHOUT MUSIC*

Black Sparrow Press-Santa Barbara-1977

ACKNOWLEDGEMENT

Some of these poems first appeared in *Adventures in Poetry, Bezoar, Big Sky, Credences, Ear in a Wheatfield, Fire Exit, Grosseteste Review, Imago, Masks, Meangin, One, This* and *Whch Way*.

A grant from the National Endowment for the Arts helped greatly during the writing of part of this book.

LIBRARY OF CONGRESS CATALOGING IN PUBLICATION DATA

Palmer, Michael, 1943-
   Without music.

   Poems.
   I. Title.
PS3566.A54W5      811'.5'4           77-22452
ISBN 0-87685-288-6 (paper edition)
ISBN 0-87685-289-4 (signed cloth edition)

*or*
*these*
*are*
*C's*
*songs*

# TABLE OF CONTENTS

# Without Music

I had a horse like that once. It went like
lightning. It was quite black. It was a
white horse. It was really dark brown, a
kind of black.

Géza Róheim, *Magic and Schizophrenia*

## For Voice

A little faithful to the dream mirror
A little faceless in the dream mirror
and followed by zeroes
how many to the head of each pin

how many to the hexagon
starry night of balancing
but of careless balancing
between identical windows

one to open one to stay closed
the figure unconscious in the leather chair
will wake up and leave
eventually, will wake up and stare

in amazement
never before having slept
Here white ones and white
ones are dancing

in particulate ones
always five to the hexagon
plus a minus equal to one
a small river lost

in thought, perfect late
nineteenth century voyage
to the bookstore and back
curved line a finger

would describe in air
Here the Pacific
meets the Sea of Cortez
to form a desert.  This is the corner

and this is the order in which we wept
six-sided tears
lovely the ironwork overhead
lovely the dome

of Montaner you showed us
in a book.  Now letter and word
have begun to disappear
the *A* no longer drawn

with three remembered strokes
but shaping itself
a little confused in the way
people conceive the possibility

as theoretical, so many feathers
to so many pounds
so many objects unidentified
will force so many witnesses

to stop their cars and watch
will cause so many dogs to bark
from the endlessly burning house
These are the toys of Dionysus

top, rattle, bone-dice and mirror
Thus farmers have nothing to eat
Thus Ocean began marriage
by wedding his sister

and Sun will never transgress his measures
lest he be found out
It's better it says to hide ignorance
We must not act and speak

as if asleep
Eye precedes ear

## Without Music 1

Too much light
means the one dimension of eleven
love inside one room and
love performing itself for two
or like this and twice

So much excitement about a new pen
leaking inconsolably
from wanting to be a column
in the Grand Hotel ('El Gran')
among tropical plants

Or the answer will be yes
to all possible versions
of the day as a container for misinformation:
the 'portable sky'; the restaurant still turning
        counter-clockwise;
on the left an arm and some heads to the right

14

The book tells its cover
that blood is thicker than bread

and the book is correct
We will grow up

to be bankers on horseback
removing our heads to say no

So I offer a beggar a stone
but a nice one

stolen from a pyramid
with broken steps

and naturally he takes it
eating the liver first

and next the legs and wings
and I respect magicians

with their triangular hearts
and the heart's measures flowing out

as a pattern
onto stone

Someone would like to dance
but afterwards says
not yet

We're beaten by a man in a three-cornered hat
until we begin to dance
Left foot to the left etc

*(for Margaret Jenkins for dancing:*
*permutations without music*
*on some seventeenth century phrases)*

The circle was the secret
The earth is the fire
The face is empty

The earth is empty
The face was the secret
The circle is the fire

The face is the fire
The earth was the secret
The circle is empty

The earth is the circle
The secret is the fire

The earth is the face
The secret is empty


The earth is the fire
The X we talked about
Nothing in its way

18

The X in its way
Nothing is the fire
The earth we talked about

Nothing we talked about
The earth in its way
The X is the fire

The X is nothing
The fire in its way

The X is the earth
The fire we talked about


The X we talked about
The face is empty
A desire of light

The face of light
A desire we talked about
The X is empty

A desire is empty
The X of light
The face we talked about

A desire is the X
Light we talked about

A desire is the face
Light is empty

How did it happen that these are Wednesdays
which keep wetting us
with tincture of mercury
until we weep
to be so taken up
and changed

         Sad tropics with priests
eating mushrooms
and ballgames played until death
sets in

         Then a silver delivery truck
to carry the winners' heads
to the Joan Crawford Bottling Plant
where we become Orange Crush
and always in demand

But entering thirdly worlds
and worlds of third

                        este cristal
this glass empties out

last night's rain
into yesterday's light

esta luz        this light
            this is

what it watches
in particular

en particular
in broken thirds

of pyramids
and mother listen

and momma listens, is that right
and sister listens if that's right

and someone under
someone in bed

remembers what hasn't been said
in necessary triplicate

And asking for difficult thirds
light blue
      and sky
           and liquid heart

under cloud
      the visible heart's
          intermittent sound

      And forgotten thirds
          Les lumières en l'air
          Me da miedo ese chorro

excellent memory
      softness
          skeletal singer

of thirds        this house
          in this forest    'why not'

And a third of a crystal equals
a third of one version of the light

When I arrived
at the mountain it was flat land

as if it had been washed out
by the sea

11:01 / 1:12
'After that comes nothing'

El animal que canta
cosas locas

Je me sauve du chant de l'hirondelle
I save myself from the swallow's song

by running down the hill. And monkeys
+ parrots = mushrooms + priests

at night, parts of particles
of phosphorous at night

and every life a clear gleam
and each one a mirror

Tomorrow meets rain. Hello
rain, hello desire, hello science

A scream sings its 3's
which try to increase

Hieroglyphics of the wrist
without music

## Without Music 2


Who is it who believes in distance
from this morning to the next

(is a question)

Deep in the shampoo museum
someone looks for darkness
related to a switch

                    A little more
of the island life
                A little more
difficult than you'd expect

The farmer takes a wife
Then what does a wife take

Master Franz Joseph
                    (Haydn)
inventing the calculus
Heidegger at Freiburg
1932             Careful nights

through Fifth Avenue windows,
                              my forty suits
of sharkskin and herringbone
for winter, my pointed beard
and cigarettes for spring

Her voice is more tuneful than her sister's (the
one of her sister)

this morning
near the six.  The black ink and the red

((one) (la azul)).  The world
of partly blue

and white but fibrous.  Or the world
of partly blue & white but fibrous

My grandfather
takes coffee with his wife

in a house in the centre
of town

where there's a square
They have two motors, six

horses and ailments
of the heart.  The king

is sitting on his palace
When will you buy my hat

The water is wet
(now but not always)

These Examples for Beginners
I eat myself up

You eat supper
.in the pure future

Beauty is magnified 14 times
Empty sleep x 14

r - r - r - r
(rr - rr - rr - rr)

The dog is an animal
The map is of Germany

Be optimistic
Señor Martinez

Mommas of crystal
skating with delicacy

El General Wéllington
El arte es inmortal

The seven colors
of red and brown

denim and leather
altitude       ignorance

equal six
discipline      quinine

brigade      lemonade
courage      pneumonia

umbrellas
the world's fattest man

Controlling the light
Controlling the flow of light

we would meet if

with one's blessings if

The Cafe Lithuania is near enough
is fairly near, is nearby if

and the logorrheic heart
this is partly in quotes

and the pyrotropic heart
like a cigarette

when you find a blue disk
or imported toy railroad car

private, containing famous baritone
who's rich, who's very almost rich

who's here to sing if
without music even if

who's rich

The death of blue weight
or look I'm listening

Evening inside
or look I'm lifting

one thing with one hand
several things with three fingers

and look he's listening
let's say bone somewhat modified

bone in the process of reorganisation
according to a model

of the final monument
to the Third International

wood, about 15'' high
figures walking in place

figures carefully located
on a balcony over water

or of course over water
The sister is weeping

My sister with her parasol
The pens and red pencil

Reading aloud is for emphasis
Reading aloud is to practice

One of one of one word
in places of here

One.  Of one of.  One word
One of one.  Of.  One word

One of one.  Of one word
We are approving of architecture

of architecture and not worried
Over there we're talking

Napoleon 1944
Painting is welcome

We're starting to have forgotten
(Timon of Athens)

Thou art the thing itself
(King Lear)

A fire storm and Good Morning
The painting is almost

We're opening a letter
Do you carefully remember

## Without Music 3

*Nomos Alpha*

It's bad luck to kill a spider
in your house
to kill a spider

crossing your table
by tallow light
if the telephone rings

you will stop writing
if the babbler speaks
or someone you love

speaks
you will stop writing
bad luck for the spider

bad luck for yourself
if you run out of ink
your writing will become invisible

and persistent
so many lives saved
from grief

in empty yucatecan hotel
on colonial square
so many hours saved

from waste
she will tell you
how many things she knows

a saline lake
recycled as art
plus a small bird

with no lower beak
plus a spider
how many myths she's learned

to insert in their original form
this one and this
one, plus one

a man in france
makes remarks about mathematics
behind a garage

le jour se lève        raises
itself        someone's been shot
twice through the heart

we will buy him another heart
and comfort his young wife
by offering cryonic images

which explain death
this is a land
decorated randomly

with mescalero cactus
you will see it once
in your life and forget it

if the needle sticks
you will stop writing
then begin again

but writing less well
each succeeding time
until assembled display embarrassment

at your ignorance of death
if a letter arrives
she will stop writing

to inspect the message
someone's been shot
twice through the heart

dottore removes the heart
and precious metals from the teeth
to avoid waste

protesting helplessness
desire to be a pianist
instead

if death comes
you will stop writing
will have stopped, writing

wishing you had done less
between interruptions
if someone crazy

across the street speaks
you will copy it down
and pretend it's your own

in order to repeat
what should have been said
why I am not a dancer

dancers jump up
and twist around
he dreamt he was a horse

that danced in time of war
this is available to perception
along with the myths

which are not available to perception
at any point on the curve
of active knowing

nightingale (very pure, with harmonics)
white-throated sparrow (clear whistle)
budgerigar (a noisy squawk

in flight)
the song
of the jungle partridge

is the purest
sounding like a flute
with no tones at all

if you go out for a walk
you'll feel the street underfoot
as you cross

## Without Music 4


The sleeper awake in his place
and a sleeper wet from rain

These chemicals which relieve us

of themselves          Señor's former body
still addressed as Señor

in the plaza.  Into
and across.  Je viens de rencontré

le vieux Pound dans un café
Je viens de rencontré

M. Picabia dans les montagnes
M. Something sur la plage

votre ami (missing friend), etc
The sleeper asleep with his cigarette

is careless about pyramids
He's worried about profiles

adjacent to a bed
Whoever can't sleep

Someone walking away from the heart's motion
will catch your attention first

causing alkaline sleep
which is colorless

except for the red
Dead imagination imagined

Imagination dead and imagined
again.  The possibility of islands

with narrow clearings for example
waterways and an azure light

meaning 450-500 range
toward the frequency where green begins

A sleeper wakes up but not too much
enough for an alphabet

and a granular light

One problem is that I can no longer bend my knee
more than 10 degrees.  But actually now I'm getting
used to the routine of moving in a different way,
sitting down with my leg straight out, etc..

Question of the clusters the

sounds make, sounds make us
including mistakes

His knee bends
10 degrees east

when north
is to his left

I'd intended to buy a color television
but picked up a Rauschenberg and a tuxedo instead

Mrs. Eleanor Gibson, while picnicking one day on
the rim of the Grand Canyon, wondered whether a
young baby would fall off.  This thought led her
to a most elegant experiment, for which she devised
a miniature and safe Grand Canyon.

The sleeper in a rosebush
As I approach the clock it stops

momentarily to honor
the beautiful lady 'swept out to sea'

yesterday at dusk
Or the clarity of a photograph

where now you identify someone
correctly as someone else

one sleeper displacing another

sleeper a little troubled
in current Pacific flood

## Tomb of Baudelaire

At the end of the bridge is a state of prison. Then
it goes back into my throat drying my throat.


Miracle of Sicilian weeping. Bleeds in one of his many
dreams.


He announced that he was about to give a free 'poetry
suicide'—a free 'poultry recital'. Everyone be-
lieved him.


\* \* \*


At the end of the bridge is a state of prison. A
voyage will hide itself in your heart, bleeding from the
left eye, the organ of sight. A voyage will hide
itself in someone unfamiliar like a heap of salt.
Mingled with the ordinary blueness would be waves of
foreheads shaped like cups.


She thought he could hear her.

41

To dance is to live.

* * *

Calm and order of an autumn sky. At the end of a
bridge is the state of prison, voyage of eye and
throat full of the fear of night. Then all of winter
will enter like a red block, or like the calm and
order of an autumn sky.

139. Change of form.  139a. Change of colour.

122. Pitfalls.  136. Covers with a lid.

* * *

It doesn't matter what you say but how you say it. By
pronouncing the words they become different. It comes
from above (pointing to his head). Then it goes all
sorts of ways down. Then it goes back into my throat
drying my throat.

Tonight it's a certainty that the President will resign
('a virtual certainty').

After the party they drove back to her house where she
sucked him off while he spoke to someone on the telephone about the possibility of a job.

42

* * *


Plato's warning against telling stories, *mython*
*tina diēgeisthai.*


Or the certainty of the ten fingers and ten feet. You
laugh a lot because during the first phase someone
who has taken hasheesh is 'gifted with a marvelous
comic sense' which contains its own opposite like the
end of a bridge.


The verb divides us evenly into two objects.


* * *


A pretty girl is like a melody.


You must be more confident now that you've won the
prize.


And if you listen. And if you listen hearing, if you
listen thought. I've been thinking about the whole
trouble about how I got lost in the woods. A man myself is lying in a house. Or alone among myself answering
a house. To be calm and voluptuous conjuring a house.
To be eligible for the house. If you listen image, if you
listen house. Ordinary calm and order of the house.
Coffee comma parentheses. Coffee parentheses order.


43

Coffee parentheses coffee.  131. Untrodden.  136. Covers
with a lid.


* * *


137. Combination.  138. Arrangement.


Plato's admonition against telling stories about
being, *mython tina diēgeisthai.*


Dear Apollinaire: We drove 500 miles to attend the
wedding of a relative.  Our son was to be in the
bridal party.  The wedding was to take place at 4 p.m.
on Saturday.  On the Friday night before the wedding,
the bride and groom got into a fight and the groom
broke the bride's nose so the wedding was canceled.
     What do we do with the wedding gift we were
going to take to the church?  Who pays for the
tuxedo our son rented for the occasion and never got
to wear?  And how about the motel bill?

## Exercises on Six

This eye that burns this light
happy to meet himself
inside herself
among selected enemies
of arterial splendor

\* \* \*

This eye that burns the light
and refuses the letter
for reasons of state

\* \* \*

The serpent poet on film
and the difficult poet on film
for a minute

\* \* \*

45

Loss of memory for a minute
in refracted light


&ast; &ast; &ast;


This eye bent over
happy to meet herself
off center


&ast; &ast; &ast;


The university poet
and the housewife poet
on film for a minute


&ast; &ast; &ast;


The arteriosclerotic poet
at his typewriter


&ast; &ast; &ast;


The doctor of poetry


&ast; &ast; &ast;

Acoustical clouds
derive their shape
from the physics of sound

## The Karakorams

*(an empty one for L.F.)*

You've heard about the Karakorams
of Central Asia

which are mountains
Multicolouredness is one

kind of complexity
in the Karakorams

and complex sleep
is the other

By negotiating the pass
we enter Kashmir

or depart from Kashmir
but never both things

at once. Inhuman storms
arrive and are gone

We fumble for our cameras
among the goatskin sacks

48

secured to the rented camels' backs
Then a sequence of clicks

indicates the accomplishment of photographs
of the pass

## Prose for Richard Dadd

What have I learned from her movement
Torn attention to gloves

A little. Sitting here a little.
While.  A kind of spelling error

carried over from childhood
and held on to

at a certain hour.  What is it
Something like one till eleven

in science fiction time
the whispered about

Martian time of green hours
that can't be made to resonate at all

through an assembled crowd
expecting the event to begin

**Texts for the Ten Days**


1


At the beginning the
heat must be hard to bear

We're not used to staring at the ceiling.  At the
end the dancers
change and go home

simply enough
even though it tends to trouble us

by professional indifference
to the various effects

I hold 300 oranges
maybe grapefruit
by the tail

for the rest of one day
At the beginning the heat

is opaque and empty
and overly considerate

of itself.  This is when you hear her

yelling in the street
where it's too dark to see

2

Yes it's true we've bitten off their heads
with great relish

Yes we've separated our fingers from our hands
as if such pleasures stemming from *yes*

were agreeable propositions
located between the space of eternal objects

which are possible
and that of actualities

which are possible machines
I believe my telephone is hemorrhaging

the result of some anxiety
in childhood, the *l*

swallowed
so that it fixes itself

between itself and *r*
such as to be unreproducible

in print
as we know it.  The escape

of blood from a vessel
warns the New World about morning

in Basic English, English
basic to an understanding

of cruel sea and light
and fire and distance

such that it's spoken face to face
by individuals numbering in the hundreds

3

This second place you enter
under mushroom umbrella

'Fire has been known to kindle itself
in otherwise darkened cellars'

This second area you enter
color added to eyes

light added to mathematics
by exponential steps

in winter weather. News
that there isn't any

to talk freely about
a sense of notoriety

like a loss of face
in the classical sense

of the term. The figure
of the child by the river

confronting reeds. Weather
and weather in winter

Hat plus shadow
Shadow of camera

4

This is your first lesson
and nothing is remembered

of elaborate exclamations
about the spine.  Not straight enough

or a little too much
or simply watch out

So-and-so removes his hands
the better to wash his feet

objectively.  Warm water
from above our bent necks

not your neck and my neck
but his necks and their head

in particular, the completely
serious way the summer days

come to be called summer nights
and/or vice versa.  How the minutes

and hours are organized
into hopeful clusters

running from smell to touch
to seconds to go.  Tentative plans

for a trip by boat
through the canal.  Wide-brimmed palm-fiber

hats, not his-and-her necks
but the sensation of ribbons

bisymmetrical, iconically candid
and heraldic.  Not possible

5

The snow everywhere and you missed it today
And the pterosaur with the wingspan
'greater than that of a phantom jet,'
seen flying over Texas
I've already started to lie. '. . . seen
flying *under* Texas,' the papers said
at a depth of 65 million years
We all missed it

6

*. . . something like a weaving or a web*
which would allow the different threads
to separate again

whenever necessary.  Afternoon
of table and light
and their opposites

the person without shame
and the person without pockets
Afternoon of flying reptiles

disappointing to live through
because boring to watch
Story of the burnt tongue

. and little story of nothing
to speak of.  I received
your letter and you've begun to reappear

in my dreams, the same house etc
but complex in a different way
than before.  Or

I received your note
and you've vanished from my thoughts
as a result

7

Grammar of clear water
from fire in hollow rock

Windowless: without rain
Ladderless: for climbing

You talk to your tongue
through a grammar made up of

mistakes: I are
You am, They

walk beside carts
We carry ourselves

between towns
We carries ourself

## Polysyndeton

Now you will have to wait
for me since I died intestate
as everyone warned

He who was getting laid, sort of
in the Boboli Gardens all along
Is it

a visceral sensation
familiar from walking around recent museums
after the passengers have escaped

through the poorly concealed fire door
The walls are more beautiful this way
and more interesting

## The Construction in the Throat

The constriction in the throat
is caused by keys
to Spain Germany France

and the Low Countries
and parts of the South
those canals where recognisable

objects float by
where the custom is always
to shake hands with yourself, unscrew

the water's lid
and drink it
We've painted our faces in several

impermissable patterns
now who will come to look
Or the translation

of that question
Suppose you're at a ballgame
and you find yourself playing

with the secret of electricity
that it's a field
and likewise not one

Inside these multiples of one
are the various and sundry ones
it's considered desirable to choke on

## Sleep and Poetry

Nervous at first
everywhere the New Young Beauties

are being discussed
and accurately photographed

and we're members of that club
which admires fenceposts

agriculture freedom and justice
Who finds a body in the street

then decides to put it on
The head more than anything

would be pleased to fit
It's a clear day of stones

Sara's Waist


He was looking in the writing (window) over a shoulder.
This coffee is naturally cold.


Behind the lack of writing (window) hangs a woolen jacket.
What she said you came for.  Something to suck all winter
around the studio.


Because of the song the corn comes up.


Essentially weightless the neighbors are desiring a new
porch.  This by way of explanation at any hour.  A bucket
for example to cure the roof.


They are to be married so we look for a mirrored wall.
I find it over a shoulder.  I'm given a choice of waters
salt or fresh and we're told to choose between the two
daughters who have already made their choice.  Would that
be Canada.

In her talking in her sleep she told a story. By the middle I was asleep he explained.

After the paint dries we will visit the Southwest, a series of invisible dots. There is a window (writing) behind my shoulder and level with their heads. Light-hearted assassination project.

By chance or conviction he had come upon, had discovered, the final letter of the alphabet, he was completely confident. First you dig a large hole. Then you fill it with smoke.

That guy sure liked house plants (speaking of Matisse).

And now the story of the Frog Princess. In the dark I search through the drawer for a blue towel (a mirrored wall).

And now the story of the Frog Princess. Outside each window (writing) ropes are hanging from the roof. Outside each door is a ladder. After the black and white period comes a time for the gradual reintroduction of color tentative at first then more assured but this is not that time.

And now the story of the Frog Princess. In what's possible
is an interim.

Outside each writing (window) she appears to stand far off.
Momma and Poppa say this tastes a) good b) ungood c)
any two of the above.

Should not the first beat of bar 45 of the opening piece
of Opus 11 be a major third

Such as fingerprints across the heart

Such as archipelagoes

The man the rain the wind off the water drove wet
covered his head


Go to the coroner and buy me a watch

## Chamber Music for Woman's Voice

The figure portrayed is portrayed by an empty chair
but the room itself is full

If she sinks to her waist in sand
will she reach water

or become water
tasting of salt

If I have the typewriter fixed
will the door pull away from its hinge

and ask to be repaired in its turn
A new denim jacket

is a gift of great value
A trip to the bank

passeth understanding
If I remember correctly

we liked the tubas best
the bass drums second best

71

and then the drum majorettes
This was before perspective

## Dance of the Bees (July)

Most people know nothing about polarized light

The scaffold is coming down
and the wind up

but the new silence laws will have a calming effect

Do you remember the winter of the stunned
        hummingbirds
he asks for the third time, how dogs can

unlearn to chase cats
and cats be taught

to ignore flowering plants
We're moving carefully backward

through the hot weather
Soon it won't quite have begun

Song

Alive in the looking out. Crossing the bridge the brakes
fail the brakes don't fail us we're not in the drink. Tell
me which sound I'd prefer to hear.

Some wind which gets brushed off, casually. Things fall and
we watch. What we love is to listen.

The great elk's unhurried eye and the chicken escaping from
its pot. Will you settle for this
                    version of winter
                            with transparent events. I have
been to Paris
and back, Paris Texas, Rome New York, Buena Vista, Beau Fleuve,
Leadville, the Hackensack Meadows, New London. Such confusion
hangs on to itself.

Or poetics: occultation, recrudescence, medieval, pneumatic,
ant and wasp, horned owls (a pair), hatred, forgetfulness,
territory, map, interval, after, solemn, metallic, numbered,
convulsive, precise. It's September. It's 1937.

The mad woman with her crutch, always happy to talk.


In the present clear blue half of us speak from underground,
indicating likenesses. We are similar to stars and lettuce,
although not as crisp. We are pale as ink, and asleep and
correct. We are Australian animals with pockets. We are not.
Are and not white and horrified, thought to thought. Are
and not breathing, correct, ornamented. Not speaking to a
cup. Not grounded in stone and wood. Not tetrahedral please.
Are and not assassins, mid-air and abstract, without shadows.
It really is raining, silent, and dry.


Seventh Symmetrical Poem, an interpolation:

The number of letters it takes
to forget our own names


The café life, sitting and screaming; or the clouded life
under both heels. Michael I liked the play very much, maybe
too much, it must have been the nakedness. Robert I'm
worried about your lower back during that long plane ride;
I hope the stop on Fiji will help. David I forgot to credit
you for the story I swallowed—forgive me, they were delicious.
And Michael (another Michael) I wonder if it wouldn't be better
not to think about the money but just to go spend August in
Maine with that painter. She even invited you.

## The Library is Burning

(Eighth Symmetrical Poem)


The library is burning floor by floor
delivering pictures from liquid to sleep

as we roll over thinking to run
A mistaken anticipation has led us here

to calculate the duration of a year
in units of aloe and wood

But there will be no more dust in corners
and no more dogs appearing through dust

to question themselves uncertainly
Should it finally be made clear

that there's no cloud inside no body
no streetlamps, no unfoldings at five o'clock

along the edge of a curved path
Masters of the present tense

greet morning from their cautious beds
while the greater masters of regret

change water into colored glass
The stirrings are the same and different

The stirrings are the same and different
and secretly the same

The fear of winter is the fear of fire
disassembling winter

and that time the message was confused
it felt the most precise

## Ninth Symmetrical Poem

(after Southwell)


It's November the thirty-third
of an actual November
and the children sleep in the crystal world
turning their heads from the fire that burns them

The burning children are invisible
but the carriers of wounded thought
are everywhere visible
as letters strung along a word

whose economies
work backward from speech
Mirrored we reflect such things
as they've seen

Dance of the Bees (August)

There comes a scream in every boy's life
in 1913
whether by coincidence or design

Dance of the Bees (September)

As the sun's
        light caught in a mirror
        or held by water . . .

To walk with bees under the earth's heel

shadowed by light
and corrected by light.  The hard sweetness sticks

to your throat
a little more each day

meaning somewhat less.  In love's presence
it's advised to go to the track

wearing love's best flowering hat
Greet royalty with a vacant smile

Greet the revolution with obvious respect
Keep your fingers to yourself

80

but display the revolution's naked wrists
Distill memory between linen sheets

Avoid all suicide pacts

## The Classical Style

It seems they never complete these things

The body flown back from Rome
Those are samples of her blood

taken from his sleeve.  Blue yes

but also white, also cylindrical
the tiles apparently brown

about four inches square
and a path worn into them

leading toward a door
or away from a door.  Now it's finished

and the cat is dead
to be replaced by another cat

cream colored with a grey mask

Only a few passages of the work are written in score
form—most of it takes the form of completely independent
instrumental parts, since the playing of the four parts is
not intended to be synchronized. 'Each player performs
his part as though he were alone.'


Certain rites performed
as with ropes hanging

from the highest trees
in the magic forest

as with light, threaded
the people said to live here

counterfeiting light

And the hooded figure circling
before the music begins, 'an

emptiness almost perfect . . .
fragile . . . precise . . . as

if an earlier
and better time had returned'


We have lost each other on the stair


We have come to listen and watch
and talk and be talked

I in my (to some) curious
elephant suit with silver studs, you

in nothing or close to nothing
at all, forming the

two of us
what they call a pair


Soon however it won't be winter
in Nebraska even though elsewhere

it will become something like winter

freezing your hand to the rail
and impeding the linear progress

of various objects
while encouraging others.  The sound

may try to slow down or at least stop
Until then we'll refuse to hear


We have lost each other on the stair in the deep snow
that forms a window.  I have visited the family in the
mountains and the village of old women and small children,
comes a storm of separate crystals winter extends as
it resists.

Among the violin cases
refrigerators, radios and dust
we are alive in these hills
or sleeping beneath a hill
Certain questions arise
Will the rains ever come
and Will the rain ever stop
You have designed the perfect house

to live in, solid
as a crystal, with
no doors or windows
and different sounds for each room
all the modern conveniences
such as light and dark
first light then dark
careful voices of the hill-dwellers

with their pointed heads
Certain questions arise
as grace notes, trills
and slides across
the broken cantus of trees
and rock
and river where it bends
as we bend ourselves


This is the shortest day of the year
when everyone can hear those sounds

This is the longest day of the year
its distance measurable as light

seen from a distance
then recorded:  Aurigula, Gemini, Taurus

Canis Major and Canis Minor
the Great Nebula and the Horse's Head

defined as a 'cloud
of cosmic dust'

spreading its relative darkness
of which we're unaware


I sometimes wonder about the response, a century from
now, to tapes or recordings of the music of today in
which the tempi are misjudged, the ensemble is sloppy,
and the rhythms have come out all wrong.  Will this
be taken as the style of our time?


That dissolution of the standard way
as this hole where there was a field
a few weeks ago, the argument concerning the mountain
lying due south, whether
to level it entirely or, the alternate idea
to remove only its crown
the top hundred feet or so
and place the houses there.  Each name

with its explanatory myth
to be studied in the regional
museum or library.  Thus Peril (Alaska),
Truth or Consequences, Bullet,

Dogtown, Natoma, Medicine Bend,
the Frying Pan and the Schuykill
Thus 'table,' 'cinema,' 'horse'
and so on, your stereoscope

in which two almost identical views
become one, whether looked at
through grey eyes or brown,
held unsteadily in either hand
the towns and rivers
appear to float, an ocean liner
crosses a wheat field explaining
that way the Great Migration

of our ancestors the hawk
and the slug, the brown eyes
with their illusion of greater depth
the grey with their impression
of pure intellect clearly separate
from emotion.  It seems
they never complete these things
the heads and arms visible

above the waves indistinctly drawn
and a possible suspension bridge
extending from the more recent past
into the less
renamed the present

## Poem Containing Two Songs

On a clear day you can't see at all
She was the second

one misremembered, clouds disturb the center of the eye

A train passes that other train
so that unmoving we begin
to drift backward, afloat—

the story everyone knows
and repeats to no one else—

afloat near an opposite shore
such as small boats
steer clear of, wondering

again at that curve
of flowered bank, the Sunday crowds
reclining or

those couples crossing the bridge
arm in arm.  The song 'Tomorrow'

for example rising like a balloon
in search of a tree

which sounds absurd but is fortunately true
and so not absurd

but part analogue to the breeze
swelling it seemed
toward two points at once, a far cry

from those late quartets
used to put cats to sleep


Europe and Asia on forgotten feet
Clouds disturb the eye's intent

A painting has been stolen
and returned, the citizen

checks his watch. You are welcome
to speak but not to talk

Europe and Asia follow
with empty sky. The first

day of spring has occured
with its warning about spring

and about first. So the fear
these houses by the water cause

is a different fear than before
Europe and Asia follow with rounded sky

The sounds increasing as they turn to light
and the light itself

the water divides.  They have come
to watch you paint

and be part of your painting
They have come to watch you paint

or to enter your painting

with open mouth, the suspended figures
seated or stretched out

across the ordered space of that 'between-world'

the island represents, the figures
both simplified and enlarged

the sails full
and the rowers frozen to their boat

They have come to enter your painting
by groups of two and three

and twos imagined as threes
and the threes that are real

but careful.  Today the city is

active, imprecise and clouded,
yesterday quiet, empty and

entire, one-fourth its own size

### Three Poems to be Read as One

The heroine will become undone, softly
filtered
light collects to one place

an arrangement of squares
on which the articles are to be placed
for inspection: one

copy of Unnatural Acts and the hand
recovered from the bottom of the sea,
a gin and lime, the Bruckner

Quartet
shows its torch.  No mind left
to make up

but a full life to look back on
So the squares
slightly shifted

would lose no interest
in themselves, his camera
pointing at them

adjusted for black
against pale brown, the speakers
are difficult to hear

* * *

who picked up the pieces of her brother's body
The owl on the mantel calls twice each day

to let you know it's alive
What otherwise could we know

about an owl, of her brother's body
the brother's feathered body

on the stone mantel,
the young sun brings sleep

in an empty bowl
to redream each day

at day's beginning, sisterly
speaking at the edge of voice

Of her brother's body
the separate parts

memory catalogues
by visible rows

the question of these trees
their orange flowers

and poisonous bark
or healing bark

and yellow flowers
Is this the week chosen by the rich

to descend into the streets and dance
or was that last week

It's always one o'clock in the afternoon
of a shadowless day

Asleep and fearing sleep
means not to wake

* * *

She has written describing the Great Emperor
's love of feathers

That will be something followed by something
less complex, childhood in Egypt

after birth at sea, colors
applied with art above each eye

as if in imitation of the Middle Eastern sky
concealing its given name

That love of conversation
causing the city to dissolve in flames

and that love of fire
telling us to watch from a hill

beyond the river.  These waist high
pink and white flowers are called mallow

and this is nightshade
Its fruit brings lasting sleep

like foxglove and oleander leaves
How carefully an ordinary

three-fingered morning
arrives, deathless and complete

in itself, unevenly
curved in shadowing itself

## The Meadow

Reassembling a meadow

The Meadow

Categorically
he would have us believe

that this isn't a language after all
that's been decoded

but something fixed
in the purpose of its telling

The Meadow

A message so to speak
limited to its function

The Meadow

. . . distinguished from a language precisely
by the invariable correlation of its signs
to the reality they signify


The Meadow


I roll off the word
in the aging process

If I had a sister
I wouldn't like her

(with good reason)
Guests on the other hand

are always provided with fresh towels
and a new bar of soap

If we go on writing books
no one will notice

And if we stop
two persons will notice

Each morning the daily paper
will be left at your door

free of charge
This is like a meadow

# The Meadow

*for Gottfried Benn*

In the hours of naming
the name of the hours

two
letters to open things

but five to unfold them
a double *t* for *tongue*

an embarkation
an accounting

a sober falling backward
(and almost upward)

with tongue doubled
to no tongue

(and almost upward
('On the song's

forehead an occasional
mirror would open'))

The Meadow

The mother explained that her four-year-old daughter
had four imaginary friends. She had grown tired of
one of them and 'killed him off,' but soon began to
miss him. Now she was bringing him back to life,
slowly, in an elaborate hospital.


The Meadow

> *for the woman who kicked her dog,*
> *breaking a toe*


The radical disinvention of butterflies
so that where they once went as escorts
the air is empty

## How they locate

Fear to enter the world
It will curl your hair


How they locate across bodies of water, where bodies cross.
In the second-person nightmare is the third. You are is it.


In the middle of the life of our life, to be awake is crystal
to be late. Roofs cover themselves. He'll fill fives
with numbers.


He'll fill cups with cups. A field has its center, here
and there. Should all of us take notes.


To be awake is crystal to be late. To be better is not a
question.


A continuous field to appear to be grey.


A provisional field to begin to appear.

100

The curtain sheds water until morning comes and I live in her letter.


Where small houses gather talking, the dismantled squares. To be awake is to be awake in rain. The way the plan never interferes (always interferes). To sleep is to be wet.


In the middle of the life of our life, fleas and cigarettes at night and careful plans at night. Cats are visible to the dark
        unlike a quick brown fox


In Worcestershire there's sauce
In New York there's junk
In Sidney there's opera
And in the known world a sense of loss


I'll trade my parrot for your potato
if you'll throw in a favorite adjective
and your country's largest river


You can never step in the same cloud twice (in the same song twice).


To cross the chicken is to cross the road.


Empty your pockets and face the camera.

To kill a carrot at 100 meters is to be accurate, but to unstring the bow and lower yourself into the hole beneath the desert which leads to paradise is to be a vegetable. Muchas gracias.

(I live in her letter.)

## On the Way to Language

The answer was
the sun, the question

of all the fragrances undressed
by the rats in the Pentagon

is Claude's, little
memory jars

empty of their pickled plums
and the tiny

pile of dried bodies under the floorboard
(we had to sell that car)

Summers are always difficult
arriving too soon, too

much wind and the absolute
darkness when it finally descends

over the plantation. We're not ashamed
of our immense wealth

even somewhat proud
of the cleanliness of the servants' quarters

From the sound of their weeping
they seem happy enough

in their work, childlike
and contrite.  The answer was

memory, an efficient
engine driven by earthly

remains and the question
of the valley of desire

crossed by the bridge
of frequent sighs

## Waltz of the Elements

I told her Marry yourself
to some other medium self

That's not what I told her


I told her Disregard the 5 of Shadows
and pick another card

which isn't what I told her


If you meet the Queen of England
a lightweight man of lyric song

disconnect his face
and replace it with your own

That's what someone told her

I'll be ready by eleven-thirty
is what she told me

That's almost what she told me


And her brother asleep between concertos
is sleeping among stones

Should that be told


Will anyone offer to tell me
whether I'd feel better

in a language of illegal regrets


It's mid-week, dry and clear
what's called 'ideal baseball weather'

part bullshit part apodeictic logic


What if all these paragraphs were assembled
and all the rest

in a sober boat
and a story were told about water

## Without Music 5


From cities the 'rivers of'

nights of eye-level          circles
                inside turnings

in messages.  Some rain soft none
melting us              Some steps

for crossing a surface


The word orange scribbled in black on a tan wall
with an arrow

to indicate direction of

shoreline          descent          'to your left'

of the body's eight directions

inside turnings, to indicate


As breakfast, ham + eggs, almost never

107

arm to enter sleeve

if the shoe fits          (care)

arm to bend gradually


As the right way of dividing up the world

into sound and more sound
Does your anguish uncloud itself

Does it hold its own hand
or doesn't it

Under liquid the parallels
afternoons we drink in

to spill out          solid

crystal of death's head
or small boy with felt hat

the messages are successive
irrepeatable acts


Fleeing it notes from a cross-fire
                    faces and shoulders

A hamburger and sand up your ass
is more like it

that is better liked,
more like, it


And the one about why do bees hum


He got up, shaved etc
caught the 8:30 bus
having forgotten to dress


Or the idea of a seasonal illness

those born in 1895 will die of
while we watch
the same event each minute

waiting for the agreed upon
signal
where certainty gets confused with evidence

leaving no doubt
This is is it a winter house
filled with the weight of numerical effects

No careful present follows
the wave of response
I think it's about 1900

and your grampa is breathing down your neck
the grampa who accomplished something

by reinventing the tree


Speaking whole sentences perfect
as a desk, its surface

               as one can sometimes

reproduce music           only
in one's inward ear           cannot

whistle it           arm at rest
horizontal           head on neck


And a car downstairs that never runs
Our burial in dust, the question of

available light
and directed light           word from England

concerning cathedrals
and public space           that the nights

these days were if anything


But to prove spring after all the too difficult
footing and lamps lit

unexpectedly. Same as the same thing
as difference. Your coffee cup has a crack

descending from its lip
and mine does not.  And in mine

the precise cigarette ends
absorbing the last of the liquid

which served in its turn to extinguish them
In love with order both of us

wondering why Brahms had a white beard
hanging below a black mustache


Time 'divided into equal parts':

                                        space     eyes
the measuring not as time

itself but a tic
of elaboration           chairs

angling walls, a direction
proposed and *therefore*

proposed as following
lightly the hours

interfere with each other
'Only the birds' she said

'clearing their throats'

And the dancers moving through stone

Same as the same thing
as difference

so that the choice of a letter
equals a (careful?) not choosing of (all?) the rest


So that a waiting between questions
equals a waiting between letters

before deciding to appear.  Adventures
in the Unknown Interior

of America.  The Seven Sermons
to the Dead


With a weather
verified by shadow

evenly colored
grey of the underleaf

as all you can see
from directly below


You fall off a bridge
holding your intestines in

and reportedly this is the moment
when others turn to crystal

the 'eye-witnesses'
enter the state of your distension

a purely gringo waltz
dedicated to liquid

first taste of coffee since the war
bread without butter and breadless

no shining plate or knife
a purely gringoid song

of arterial splendor
in quotes

## Without Music 6

(A Book of Rhetoric in Big Sur)

The friendship of moths will be real
as inhabiting a green house is real

as green and living seem equal
as the habit is equal to itself

The women who lived here
talked to themselves the men

are undressing to play cards
Subtract all numbers from the letter d

and we've lost our feet
Let one and letter be equal

## Night of the Full Moon: the Etudes: a Woman
## Claps her Hands

Les vacances so to speak brief
They have visited themselves as

visitors, one flower finished, another
just as suddenly they are are

we not discussing *sky,* clouded
and inhabiting

such chapters as
'The Glass Door'

'The Clerodendron'
or bleeding heart

Through this window the jade house
can be seen.  They are naked

and asleep
and known as enraptured

between perfect tablets
This rain is unseasonable

but welcome


This rain is unseasonable but welcome
We are tired of it

and wish it would stop
among the houses of government

of which the jade house is one
We are tired and wish we could stop


Above the harbor the Magellanic light
floats, deceiving visitors

Each stone is measureless and fixed
against stone.  Each letter arriving

is opened, and Hermolaus Barbarus
sits in one place at one time

next to Abelard and William of Champeaux
and the previous morning's sun


Cries (she cries) from the darkened corridor
Look they have stolen my jaw

They have stolen my lower jaw—
dreamt in broad afternoon light—

The idea arises as icon
Someone solemn portrayed

claims to remember that Etrurian landscape
of empty messages.  Sung this is a song

if spoken, more trees
and clear lakes into turnings, the precise

invisible spirals will cross
mimicking roads

## Dutch Graves in Bucks County

She opens the letter and looks off stage

The theme of Christian sacrifice is prominent
in our dreams
as prominent as we please

There's less content here
but more activity
more rings on fingers

than in fashion magazines
more cocks and cunts showing
than in our dreams

The costume was unraveling
and the star thought to explain

in order to draw the audience's attention away
from their dreams

She opens the letter and glances off stage

Her costume is unraveling
and the star decides to explain
about the play

## Tenth Symmetrical Poem

A dream in imperfect alexandrines
Through night's eye those tending the book move
as surds or signs, the cooks with their guns
and soldiers with their aprons and copper pots
define archē and telos, passages

translucent as
the old Stalinist says
dolphins in their course, the forest is
hazardous, 'familiar,' its hidden
events.  Through night's eye those tending the

book peer out
on a scene from a book
while we who have been translated
(who are waiting to be translated)
do not

## Symmetrical Poem

(eleventh—speaking)


Dragon lady raises cigarette to painted lips
Midnight perfect artifice such wars begin or was it
end, tomorrow's
light and more light, 'I know

that that's a tree,' spreading and
broad-leaved, at times a house
or street or city made of glass
in which a city can be seen

What did he want to do. Let me show you this photograph
of an actual camera cut in half
Some of them talk then, light
to filter other light

across those figures joining hands
the tortoise, triangle and iris
the rowers, the goat and the ram
familiar as mathematics

such languages where things follow
charged and enclosed
the 'hills narrowly ranged'
through which the riders pass

121

## Without Music

*Les lettres qui formaient des mots artificiels*

—Reverdy

Small sun against the lower edge licking us
She showed me her tongue coated with thorns

A careful life of stars in a redwood box

times labor's loss not mine
based upon the loss itself, 'not mine'

. . . formed such words imperfectly bodied

as empty sleep weighed against dream
bodies and parts of bodies distributed

according to given laws
across a field
Who could help but love the equations

night's music hung from each line
the headless man looks at the quarter moon

122

and the moon watches the man
resting invisible beneath a tree

*luminous city*        sounds that pour
from the center of a courtyard

where we watch ourselves talk
This poem is called Rebuilding the House

## Crossing the Hill

*for A.M.*

Queens and kings of the perilous edge
of an alphabet we
are are we this
faithful cat crossing the hill

to where time sits
in its midday likeness
or ordinary dark time
like an alphabet

dancing the straight-forward dance
Egypt lives in certain cats
who refuse to scratch
and refuse to sit

here where Egypt lives
as an alphabet
of visible undertakings
mistaken for an actual cat

who is the opposite of an alphabet
geometrical and abstract
and alive because of that
How long will the dry time last

124

beneath the hill
the serious speakers ask
have the makers unbuilt all this
to decorate a hill

# Cloud Forms

*for Jean Arp*

It's the end of another century when light prematurely
divides. We are lit seriously brown in our baths, a
color actually closer to mauve. We are lit by old-
fashioned lamps, their curved light falling across a
field designed with random holes. The time when each
one of us on a baseball team is neither nominalist nor
realist but simply uncertain of what the words mean.
I for example have reintroduced the art of continuous
revision of the scorecard until it resembles a palimpsest
of possible games. You remain content to bang out hits,
mostly to left. Others pop up. What's the difference.
The one between sitting and standing is one, the only
one I can think of. Peter this isn't cricket and wishes
won't make it so. I've hit someone in the head again
with the ball, but was it my fault for throwing or his
for being in the way. Jack get up. I've widowed his
lovely wife who studies ballet. Her children will
starve since there's no money to be made from ballet,
except by the unfortunate few who began too young and had
various important parts of their wills removed. The

part of my will that was removed returns for brief
moments, though I'm not sure which part it was. I think
the upper part. When it returns I argue about cause and
effect, not caring for either one but hopeful that
a third term might be invented to describe the process
of going on. When it disappears I grow silent and still
another kind of cloud forms.

## The Meadow

*for Robert Duncan*

Resembling a meadow
'folded in all thought'
a lamp is lit only vaguely remembered
for its form, an elephant
of pale blue porcelain
with trunk curved upward
lighting a room        a gift
toward a featureless room
whose walls are lined with children's books
whose readers are unable to read

Printed July 1977 in Santa Barbara & Ann Arbor
for the Black Sparrow Press by Mackintosh and Young
& Edwards Brothers Inc. Design by Barbara Martin.
This edition is published in paper wrappers;
there are 200 hardcover copies numbered & signed
by the author; & 26 copies handbound in boards by
Earle Gray lettered & signed by the author.

*Photo:* Tom Webster

Michael Palmer was born in 1943 in New York City (down the block from the Gotham Book Mart). While at Harvard College edited *Joglars* with Clark Coolidge. Undergraduate thesis on writings of Raymond Roussel. 1966-68 did graduate work at Harvard (M.A., Comparative Literature) before moving to San Francisco in the fall of 1969. His publications include *Plan of the City of O, Blake's Newton, C's Songs, The Circular Gates, Relativity of Spring* (with Geoffrey Young, translations from the poetry of Vicente Huidobro), and *Without Music.* In 1974 he received a grant from the National Endowment for the Arts. While living in San Francisco he has worked with several contemporary composers and for the past three years has collaborated on a number of dance pieces with Margaret Jenkins and the Margaret Jenkins Dance Company.